The Ringing of the BELL

by: Marinda W. Lane

illustrated by Myke Irving

To order additional copies of this book, contact:
Xlibris
844-714-8691
www.Xlibris.com
Orders@Xlibris.com

ISBN: 979-8-3694-1886-4 (sc)
ISBN: 979-8-3694-1888-8 (hc)
ISBN: 979-8-3694-1887-1 (e)

Library of Congress Control Number: 2024906173

Print information available on the last page

Rev. date: 04/09/2024

This book is dedicated to my brother, Darrell. Thanks for all the fun memories growing up in the country and always looking out for me. There's nothing like playing in the creek on a hot summer day. Love you!

Yes he still is playing in creeks just on a bigger scale with big equipment. He has been working with streams and rivers all around the U.S.

In the warm days of Summer, Luke and Emily were busy doing their chores on the farm. Luke fed and watered the cows, while Emily gathered the eggs. Today she had five in her basket. To finish, Luke swept up the barn hay he dropped, and Emily played with Butterscotch, the barn cat. Their yellow lab, Maggie, was laying at the front of the barn door with her eyes closed taking a little nap.

Now that their chores were done, the rest of the day was left to go to their favorite place, the creek. There they could spend endless hours playing in the cool shady woods while the water slowly wound around the edge of the banks.

Outside the barn was a tall cedar wood pole with an old black iron bell at the top. The long string hung down from the bell where it hooked onto a nail. Whenever Luke and Emily were to come home, their parents rang the bell. The bell was only rung when necessary, not for fun.

Emily took the basket of eggs to her mom as Butterscotch followed her to the house.

"I got five eggs today mom," she shouted through the door.

As her mom opened the glass door to get the basket, Butterscotch ran right into the house.

"We are going to the creek okay mom?" Emily said as she ran off the porch missing the last two steps, while Luke waited by the bell.

Mom said, "Have fun and we will ring the bell when it is time to come home. Luke, look after you sister."

"Yes, ma'am," said Luke.

Luke and Emily crossed the wooden fence and raced through the wheat field towards the woods. The wheat was up to their waist. It was brown, almost ready to pick and tickled their legs as they were running through it.

Not far into the woods was what they like to call their creek. Of course, Maggie was ahead of them. She knew exactly where they were going, and she loved the water. You could see her head come up and out of the wheat as she ran.

Down by the creek, Luke and Emily took turns swinging on a long white rope tied to an old oak limb that had grown across the creek. Their dad had put several knots in the rope for gripping. Back and forth across the creek they would swing screaming with excitement as it tickled their tummies. Sometimes they would let go and splash down in the water.

As the day went on, Luke and Emily were busy as little beavers building themselves a dam across the water. They had gathered rocks along the edge of the creek bank and carefully placed them in a row along with sticks. Then, they would pack mud and clay on top. It was exciting to see the water begin to back up and get deeper behind the dam.

"It's holding the water back and filling up isn't it, Emily?" Luke said.

Emily replied, "It sure is and this one is going to be a good one."

As they continued to build the dam taller, they added a long 2-inch black pipe as an overflow and packed more mud around it. Luke had borrowed it from his dad's tool shed. His dad let him keep it at the creek. It was so neat to see the water start trickling through the pipe. The water made a small waterfall that splashed onto a pile of rocks Emily had placed under the pipe's end. Both Emily and Luke stood back proudly looking at what they had built.

They both enjoyed playing in the creek with the cool wet water on their feet and hands. Even Maggie had laid down in the middle of the creek to cool herself in the deeper water.

As the day passed on, Emily and Luke played. Emily found some clay on the edge of the water and decided to mold teacups and plates. She loved to feel the soft, cool, squishy gray clay on her hands.

Luke played with Maggie up and down the creek. Maggie would run and splash with a stick in her mouth. When she got tired, she would plop down in the water.

Emily noticed a breeze picking up. The leaves on the branches began to rustle and dance in the wind.

She looked up and said to Luke, "Are we expecting a storm today?"

"No," said Luke, "It is just the wind blowing. Don't worry."

Emily looked at Luke and then back up to the sky. She trusted her brother and began working on her clay bowls again. Before long, the dark gray clouds began to roll in. The sun slowly disappeared behind the clouds.

Maggie stood up in the creek and shook herself off. She ran up on the bank sniffing all around, even the air, as if she were now a hunting dog on a major hunt.

In a concerned voice Emily asked again, "Are you sure it is not going to storm? Look at the sky, it looks dark, and the wind is getting stronger. I think we should go home."

Luke replied, "Don't be such a scaredy cat. If it is going to storm, mom will ring the bell."

By now the trees swayed and thunder rumbled in the distance. Emily felt her heart beating a little faster and her stomach in knots. She was too afraid to walk home by herself, so she decided to wait on a log on the edge of the bank. She rubbed Maggie on the head, while she listened ever so closely for the bell.

A rumble of thunder made Emily jump and say, "Luke, come on! Let's go! It is getting closer!"

Luke replied in a stern voice. "I'm almost finished with the touchups on our dam and this time I think it will hold even if it rains a lot."

Finally, between the rumbles of thunder, they heard the bell ring, "ding, ding, ding." Sounding just like an old church bell. Emily jumped to her feet and Luke ran up the bank out of the creek. They both took off running with Maggie on their heels. The bell continued ringing as they ran out of the woods. Luke and Emily ran as fast as they could through the swaying wheat fields to get home. Emily felt her legs burning as she ran. She did not want to be left behind. Maggie was now way ahead of them both. The sky was almost black as if it were late in the evening. The air smelt of rain too.

Luke and Emily could see their dad standing at the barn door waiting. They could not wait to get to him. When they finally reached the barn, both Luke and Emily bent over to catch their breath.

As dad looked up at the spinning windmill and the dark clouds in the sky, he said, "Looks like this storm is going to be a big one. We'd better get to the house. Mom's probably waiting."

The storm raged outside. Thunder rolled through the hills and lightning flashed. The wind steadily beat rain against the windows. Emily still jumped at the sound of thunder. She was safe now next to her parents. They sat around the table, eating a nice snack, while Maggie curled up on her bed and Butterscotch on the back of the couch. Luke told his mom and dad how the dam was built and how he couldn't wait to see if it held from all the rain. Emily was also excited talking about the bowls and plates she had made. She was going to make enough for a creek tea party. However, she figured they would be ruined by the storm, and she would have to start over. Of course, they talked about swinging on the rope and playing with Maggie.

As Emily ate her peanut butter and jelly sandwich, she told her mom and dad, "I hope next time when the air begins to stir, and clouds start moving in, Luke listens to me a lot sooner!"

Luke just rolled his eyes and said, "She's just a scaredy cat mom."

He then looked at her and asked, "But aren't you ready to go back to our creek?"

Emily replied, "I sure am!"

Luke and Emily's dad said, "We will always ring the bell when it is time to come home."

This is Marinda's bell growing up. Unfortunately
the farm or the bell are no longer there.

Printed in the United States
by Baker & Taylor Publisher Services